A NOTE TO PARENTS

When your children are ready to "step into reading," giving them the right books is as crucial as giving them the right food to eat. **Step into Reading Books** present exciting stories and information reinforced with lively, colorful illustrations that make learning to read fun, satisfying, and worthwhile. They are priced so that acquiring an entire library of them is affordable. And they are beginning readers with a difference—they're written on five levels.

Early Step into Reading Books are designed for brand-new readers, with large type and only one or two lines of very simple text per page. **Step 1 Books** feature the same easy-to-read type as the Early Step into Reading Books, but with more words per page. **Step 2 Books** are both longer and slightly more difficult, while **Step 3 Books** introduce readers to paragraphs and fully developed plot lines. **Step 4 Books** offer exciting nonfiction for the increasingly independent reader.

The grade levels assigned to the five steps—preschool through kindergarten for the Early Books, preschool through grade 1 for Step 1, grades 1 through 3 for Step 2, grades 2 through 3 for Step 3, and grades 2 through 4 for Step 4—are intended only as guides. Some children move through all five steps very rapidly; others climb the steps over a period of several years. Either way, these books will help your child "step into reading" in style!

http://www.randomhouse.com/

Library of Congress Cataloging-in-Publication Data
Berenstain, Stan, 1923–
The Berenstain bears big bear, small bear / by Stan & Jan Berenstain.
   p.   cm. — (Step into reading) (An early step-into-reading book)
SUMMARY: The Bear family demonstrates the difference between big and small with a variety of objects from hats and heads to suits of clothes.
ISBN 0-679-88717-2 (trade). —ISBN 0-679-98717-7 (lib. bdg.)
[1. Size—Fiction. 2. Bears—Fiction.] I. Berenstain, Jan, 1923 –. II. Title. III. Series.
IV. Series: Early step-into-reading.
PZ7.B4483Bemjf 1998
[E]—dc21
97-36284

Printed in the United States of America   10 9

Early Step into Reading™

The Berenstain Bears
BIG BEAR
SMALL BEAR

Stan & Jan Berenstain

Random House 🏠 New York

Big bear.

Small bear.

Small hat,
big head.

Big hat,
small head.

Too small.

Too big.

Just right!

Just right!

One big.

One small.

Small suit,
big bear.

Big suit,

small bear.

Too tight.

Too loose.

Just right!

Just right!

One big.

One small.

Big bear,
small seat.

Small bear,

big seat.

Too heavy.

Too light.

Just right!
Just right!

One big.

One small.

Small bowl,
big bear.

Big bowl,

small bear.

Too little.

Too much.

Big bowl,
big bear.

Small bowl,
small bear.

Just right!

Just right!